SONG
OF
THE
RIVER

Written by Joy Cowley

Illustrated by Kimberly Andrews

GECKO PRESS

Cam the mountain boy said to his grandfather,
"I wish I could see the sea."
"One day we will go there," said his grandfather.

One spring morning, Cam was playing by his house.
He watched a trickle of water running through the pine trees.
The water splashed and sang in the voice of snow,
"Come with me. Come with me. I will take you to the sea."

Cam followed the trickle of water in and out of the trees. It joined other trickles and became a creek.

"Are you going to the sea?" Cam asked.
The creek laughed down the mountainside
and chattered over stones.
It sang in the voice of a waterfall,
"Yes, yes. Come with me. I will take you to the sea."

The creek met another creek and became a rushing
stream, which combed the hair of reeds and ferns
and hid a thousand little fishes between its banks.

It sang to Cam in the voice of leaping trout,
"Come with me. Come with me."
And Cam shouted in reply, "We are going to the sea."

Near the bottom of the mountain the stream became a river.
It flowed through farms where ducks swam and cows drank and dogs
barked and a farmer took his cream to the town in a small boat.
Cam said to the river, "You haven't changed your mind, have you?"

The river sang in the voice of green and gold frogs,
"We will go, you and me. I will take you to the sea."

The river drank in other rivers and became wider, deeper.
It went under bridges and alongside roads and railway tracks.
It carried a paddleboat full of people on a picnic.
And all the time, it sang of the sea in the voice
of big brass engines soaked in oil.

After a while, the river became so wide
that Cam could barely see the other side.
The near bank was fenced with factories
and wharves with ropes and cranes like
sky ladders and tall ships and small ships
and rusty barges and trusty tugboats.

There was so much noise that Cam could
no longer hear the song of the river.
He sighed and sat down.
"You're too busy to go anywhere," he said.

Then the river began to sing in a new, loud voice—
the voice of salty wind and crying birds and deep,
secret places where whales swam with their young.
"Come with me!" the river called.

Cam got up and ran, past the wharves,
along the road and over some sand dunes.

In front of him was the sea.
It was wild and blue and beautiful. . .
and it went on forever.

Cam ran down the beach and splashed his feet
in the waves as they ran up the sand.

The sea sang him a song about a salty wind and
crying birds and deep, secret places where whales
give birth to their young, and wharves with cranes
and ships with cargoes and big brass engines and
green and gold frogs and leaping trout and a waterfall
and—yes—in a faint whisper, it sang of snow.

When Cam went home to the mountain,
he said to his grandfather, "I saw the sea."
"One day we will go there," said his grandfather.

That night, Cam went out under the stars.
He cupped his hands in the trickle of water.
"Why didn't you tell me you were the
beginning of the sea?" he asked.

To my parents, Janet and Simon—thank you for my
perfect childhood in the Canadian Rockies.—KA

This edition first published in 2019 by Gecko Press
PO Box 9335, Wellington 6141, New Zealand
info@geckopress.com

Text © Joy Cowley 1994
Illustrations © Kimberly Andrews 2019
© Gecko Press Ltd 2019

Gecko Press acknowledges the generous support of Creative New Zealand

ARTS COUNCIL OF NEW ZEALAND TOI AOTEAROA

Design and typesetting by Vida Kelly
Printed in China by Everbest Printing Co. Ltd,
an accredited ISO 14001 & FSC-certified printer

ISBN hardback: 978-1-776572-53-3
ISBN paperback: 978-1-776572-54-0

For more curiously good books, visit geckopress.com